Bases are loaded . . . in more ways than one.
Find out why in
STOLEN BASES

Who's at the screen of the crime?
Get the answer in
MODEM MENACE

A trip into the wilderness can get pretty wild!
See why in
TERROR TRAIL

Here's a job that will really haunt you.
Check out
GRAVE DISCOVERY

It's time to face the music! Take a look at
SEE NO EVIL

Who's *really* behind the wall?
See for yourself in
A BONE TO PICK

Who's calling? Get the answer, read
PLEASE CALL BACK!

Somebody's inside . . . but nobody should be.
See who in
ANYBODY HOME?

Shop . . . until you drop!
Read all about it in
BUYING TROUBLE

7 8 9 01 00

Produced by Mega-Books of New York, Inc.
Design and Art Direction by Michaelis/Carpelis Design Assoc.

Cover illustration: Ken Spencer

HOME, CREEPY, HOME

by Joanne Barkan

interior illustrations by
Marcy Ramsey

STECK-VAUGHN
ELEMENTARY · SECONDARY · ADULT · LIBRARY

A Harcourt Company

www.steck-vaughn.com

CHAPTER ONE

"Home, sweet home!" Wesley Cobb announced. He stepped back from the wall he was painting. "This place is looking good!" He jabbed his twin brother Everett with the handle of his paint roller.

Ev jabbed him back. "Right," Ev agreed. "And you know the best thing about this new apartment, Wes? I won't be sharing a bedroom with *you* anymore."

Mr. and Mrs. Cobb were sanding the wood mantel. Mrs. Cobb looked up. "Keep painting, guys," she said. "We have just one week to finish everything. Then it's moving day."

The Cobbs had always wanted to live in one of the elevator apartment buildings on Prospect Drive. Now, finally, their dream had come true.

"Speaking of moving, who will help me move this?" asked Mr. Cobb. He pointed to the huge painting hanging over the mantel. It showed a group of people waiting for a bus.

Wes looked at the painting's wood frame. "The frame is bolted into the wall," he said.

"So, unbolt it," Ev told Wes. "That is one ugly painting!"

"I like it," said Mrs. Cobb. "It's about real people going to work. It belonged to the woman who lived in this apartment before us. She was almost ninety when she died."

"Yeah, I think it's a pretty cool picture," added Wes.

Just then the phone rang. The phone was on the floor near the window. Ev answered it.

"Cobb family," Ev said. Then he slammed down the phone. "The person hung up! This is the third time that's happened. It's driving me crazy!"

"It's a new phone number—" Mr. Cobb began. The sound of the doorbell cut him off.

"What is this, Central Station?" Wes muttered. He jogged to the door and opened it.

The building superintendent, Frank Tella, stood in the hall. He nodded at Wes without smiling.

"I just wanted to tell you folks something," said Frank. "Don't make noise after ten o'clock."

"No problem," Mrs. Cobb answered.

Frank peered inside the door. He nodded again. "My brother and his family would have loved this

8

apartment," he said. Then he turned and walked down the hallway.

Wes shut the door and rolled his eyes. "Weird," was all he said.

"But he seems like a good super," said Mr. Cobb.

Before anyone could say anything, the doorbell rang again.

"It's your turn," Wes said to Ev.

Ev opened the door. A young woman stood in the hall. She looked tired.

"I'm Lisa Chu," she said. "I live right downstairs. I heard noise in this apartment. So I decided to see what was going on. I didn't know this place had been rented."

Mr. Cobb came to the door. "Hello there," he said. "I hope we haven't disturbed you."

Lisa sighed. "I work in the evenings. I try to rest during the day," she explained.

Mr. Cobb nodded. "We'll try to make less noise. And once we move in, we'll have carpets on the floors. That should help a lot."

Lisa thanked Mr. Cobb. Then she headed for the elevator.

"What's next? A telegram?" joked Wes.

Ev laughed. He was still laughing when the phone rang again. He picked it up and said, "Funny farm here. Corn on the Cobbs."

"Everett!" Mr. Cobb said sharply. He reached for the phone. Then he stopped. His tone changed. "What's wrong, Ev?" he asked.

Ev's eyes were twice as large as usual. "There was someone there this time," Ev said, his voice shaking. "It was a weird, horrible voice."

"What did the voice say?" Wes asked.

Ev took a deep breath. "The voice said, 'Get out of that apartment or you'll all get hurt!' " Ev gasped.

CHAPTER TWO

Mr. and Mrs. Cobb looked at each other. "It's got to be someone who knows we're working in here," said Mr. Cobb. "But who would do such a thing? And why?"

"How about Frank Tella?" asked Wes. "Maybe he wants to rent this apartment to other folks who'll pay him lots of money."

"It could be Lisa Chu," said Ev. "Maybe she's a quiet freak. Maybe she doesn't want upstairs neighbors at all."

"Let's quit work for today," said Mrs. Cobb. "We'll go back to the old apartment and make dinner. Tomorrow we can start here fresh."

The next morning, everyone felt better. They got to the building on Prospect Drive around nine o'clock.

"Let's finish up the living room," Mr. Cobb said as they stepped into the elevator. At the fifth floor, Wes was the first one out.

"Yo, Ev," he said. "Hand me the . . ." His voice broke off. Then suddenly he was shouting. "Look at this mess! What total jerk did this?"

The entire hall near their apartment was covered with shredded newspaper.

"Look!" called Ev. "There's something taped to the front door. It looks like a fortune from a fortune cookie."

Ev pulled the fortune from the door. " 'When you see danger, get out of its way,' " he read.

"I don't like this one bit," Mr. Cobb muttered. He opened the apartment door with his key.

"Let's get this stuff into the garbage," said Mrs. Cobb. She picked up an armload of newspaper. Ev did the same. He followed his mother down the hall.

They found an empty plastic bag in the janitor's closet.

"This is one of Frank Tella's bags," said Ev. "He uses these bright orange kind."

Ev opened the bag. A second later, he threw it down angrily. "Frank did all this!" he shouted. "Look in the bag, Mom. There are a bunch of newspaper shreds at the bottom!"

Ev and Mrs. Cobb hurried back down the hall. Mr. Cobb was still clearing away the newspaper mess.

"We know who's guilty," declared Ev. "It's Mr. Quiet-Please himself, Frank Tella!"

"Now wait a minute," said Mrs. Cobb. "We don't know for sure."

"Mom," Ev said impatiently. "We know that he . . ."

Just then they heard Wes shouting.

"It's Wes!" cried Ev.

"It sounds like he's in the back of the apartment!" said Mr. Cobb.

CHAPTER THREE

Ev and his parents raced through the apartment. They found Wes standing near the back bathroom. He had one hand on his stomach. He held his nose with the other hand.

"Take a whiff," Wes gasped. He pointed to the bathroom.

They all poked their heads inside.

"Gross!" said Ev. "What is that smell?"

"It's rotting garbage," answered Mrs. Cobb. "But where is it?"

"There's an air vent in the ceiling," said Wes. "Let's check it out."

Wes used a stepladder to reach the vent. He unscrewed the grill that covered it. "I don't believe it!" he yelled.

"Someone hung a stinking garbage bag in here!"

Wes pulled down the bag. Mr. Cobb insisted on looking inside it. "Food," he said. "Rotting Chinese food."

Ev groaned. "And we already know what happened to the fortune cookie," he said.

17

"Frank Tella strikes again," declared Ev. "Does he have a key to this apartment?"

"I don't know," said Mrs. Cobb.

"Maybe he did it from outside," suggested Wes. "This air shaft must have another opening."

Ev and Wes dashed out of the bathroom past their parents. In minutes, they'd found the other air vent. It was in the hall near the back stairs. Wes checked the screws on the grill.

"The paint is all chipped," Wes said.

"Yeah, because someone removed the grill," said Ev. "Frank's the one. Who else would know about the vent in our bathroom?"

"Someone who has the same kind of apartment on another floor, like Lisa Chu. Or like all the people above and below us," Wes explained. "We need some hard facts, Ev. It's time for some expert detective work."

The boys checked in with their

parents. Then they headed down to the lobby.

"Let's try the mailroom first," said Wes. "Everyone goes through the mailroom. Maybe we can find out more about Lisa Chu."

The boys inspected their own mailbox. They read everything on the bulletin board. They stared at everyone who walked by. One man stared back.

"Are you the new tenants?" he asked.

"I'm Ev Cobb. This is my brother Wes," said Ev. "We're moving in on the fifth floor."

"I'm Professor Ty Walsh," said the man. He shook hands with them. "I teach art history at the college. How do you like your new home?"

"We like it," said Wes. "But I'm not sure it likes us. I mean, we've made too much noise for our neighbor, Lisa Chu. Do you know her?"

"Ah, Miss Chu. Yes," said Professor Walsh. "She's the young woman who

works in a Chinese restaurant," he added.

"She works in a Chinese restaurant?" exclaimed Ev.

Wes elbowed his brother in the ribs. "She told us she works evenings and rests during the day," Wes said to Professor Walsh.

Professor Walsh nodded. He pulled mail out of his box. "Right," he said. "It's best to be as quiet as possible." He nodded again as he left the mailroom. "Well, nice meeting you," he added.

Ev looked at Wes. Then Ev counted off the clues on his fingers: "Chinese restaurant. Chinese food. Fortune cookie. Same kind of apartment," he said.

"Let's go!" shouted Wes.

Ev and Wes didn't wait for the elevator. They raced up the stairs to the fifth floor.

"Wait till Dad and Mom hear this!" said Ev. He stopped to catch his breath. Then the boys raced down the hall to their apartment. Just as Wes reached for the doorknob they heard a loud crash.

Wes froze. "That sounded like smashed glass!" he cried.

CHAPTER FOUR

"Mom! Dad!" Ev shouted as he and Wes rushed into the apartment.

The living room was empty. The boys dashed into their parents' bedroom. Mr. and Mrs. Cobb were there. The floor was covered with broken glass from the tall window. In the middle of the glass lay a large rock.

Mrs. Cobb pointed to the fire escape that ran past the broken window. "Our visitor waited until this room was empty," she said. "Then he tossed the rock from there."

"Maybe *she* tossed it and then ran down the fire escape to *her* apartment," said Wes.

Ev carefully picked up the rock. He turned it over in his hand. "There's no message on it," he said.

Mr. Cobb frowned. "I think the message is pretty clear—get out! And I'm ready to listen. We can find an apartment somewhere else. This place has really bad vibes for me," he muttered.

"For me, too," Mrs. Cobb agreed.

"You can't cave in," Wes declared. "We've got to fight back!"

Mrs. Cobb sighed. "Let's clean up this glass and go home. We'll talk about it later, in a safe place," she suggested.

That evening, Mr. and Mrs. Cobb went out to visit some of their friends. Ev and Wes stayed home with a stack of video tapes.

"So what do we watch?" asked Wes. "A gross horror flick or a brainless comedy?"

Ev looked at his brother. "I have another story on my mind," he said. "And it's called . . ."

" 'Home, Creepy Home,' " said Wes. "Right?"

Ev grinned. "Yeah," he answered. Then Ev got serious. "I bet our new apartment will be hit again tonight. We should be there to catch the creep," he added.

Ten minutes later, Ev and Wes were biking up Prospect Drive. Twenty minutes later, they unlocked the back door of their new apartment. The

apartment was dark.

"Head for the dining room," whispered Wes. "And don't use the flashlight."

The boys felt their way to a corner of the room. They sat down on the floor and waited.

"Frank Tella will come in the back door," whispered Ev. "He'll use his key."

"Lisa Chu will use the fire escape," said Wes. "She'll come in through the broken window."

A half hour went by.

"Man, I'm bored," whispered Ev. "I'm falling asleep."

"Sh-sh," ordered Wes. "I hear something!"

"That's me snoring," Ev shot back.

Wes jabbed Ev in the ribs. Then they both heard it: a soft thud followed by quiet footsteps. The footsteps moved across their parents' bedroom and into the living room. Ev gripped the flashlight. The boys stood up slowly. They listened.

"Come on!" whispered Wes.

Wes and Ev inched along silently toward the living room. They reached the wide entry. In the dark they could just make out a figure near the mantel. Wes nodded to Ev. Ev switched on the flashlight.

The figure whirled around and was blinded by the light. It was Professor Ty Walsh!

"What the . . ." Walsh shouted. He squinted into the light. Then he suddenly bent down. He grabbed something off the floor—a crowbar! Swinging the crowbar wildly, Walsh charged at the boys.

CHAPTER FIVE

"Watch out!" Wes yelled to Ev.

Ev ducked just in time. Walsh swung again. He knocked the flashlight out of Ev's hand. Walsh raised the crowbar for another swing.

Suddenly there was a noise at the front door. A key turned in the lock. The door swung open. Mr. and Mrs. Cobb and Frank Tella stood in the hall.

"Hey! What's going on?" Mr. Cobb demanded.

Ty Walsh threw down the crowbar. He started to run out of the room.

"I'll get him!" Ev screamed. He made a flying leap and tackled Walsh. Mr. Cobb quickly pinned down Walsh by the shoulders.

Mrs. Cobb ran to the phone. Her voice was loud and clear. "Get me the police!" she cried.

Frank Tella looked shocked. He stood over Walsh. "What are you doing here?" he asked.

Walsh stared at the painting over the mantel. He said just one word: "Lansky!"

The next morning, Ev and Wes sat on the living room floor in the new apartment.

"I'm starving," said Ev. He looked at all the food spread out on the picnic blanket.

"Don't even think about it," warned Wes. "We're waiting for Mom and Dad to get back from the police station. Then we'll eat."

Just then, the door opened. Mr. and Mrs. Cobb walked in. Minutes later, four very hungry people were munching away.

"By the way, guys," said Mrs. Cobb. "You shouldn't have come to the apartment alone last night. You're lucky we came home early and guessed where we'd find you."

"Well, we won't have to do it again, now that Walsh was caught," said Ev. "But who's this Lansky guy he was talking about?"

"Samuel Lansky was an artist," explained Mr. Cobb. "He painted working people. He died in the 1930s. He wasn't famous when he was alive. But a few years ago, his work was discovered. Now his paintings are worth lots of money."

"And that's one of them?" asked Wes. He pointed to the painting hanging over the mantel.

Mrs. Cobb nodded. "Professor Walsh

wanted that painting. The woman who lived here wouldn't sell it to him. So when she died, Walsh decided to steal it. But we rented the apartment before he had a chance."

"So Walsh was trying to drive us out!" exclaimed Wes.

"And he tried to make Lisa Chu and Frank Tella look guilty," Ev added. "Right?"

"You've got it," sighed Mr. Cobb.

"And now the painting is ours?" asked Wes.

Mrs. Cobb shook her head. "No. It's going to the art museum. We'll have an empty space above the mantel. What should we put there?" she asked.

Ev grinned. "A big sign that says . . ." he began.

Wes rolled his eyes. "Home, Sweet Home!"